goes to bed

Colin and Jacqui Hawkins

Collins
An Imprint of HarperCollins*Publishers*

Foxy got ready for bed. He had a bath, put on his pyjamas and brushed his teeth.

"I'm so sleepy," said Foxy as he climbed into bed. But his little sister couldn't get to sleep.

Foxy tucked his little sister back into her bed.
"I'll read you a story," he said. "*Once upon a time...*"
"Zzzz!" Soon his little sister was fast asleep.

"I need a drink now," said Foxy. And he went to get a glass of water.

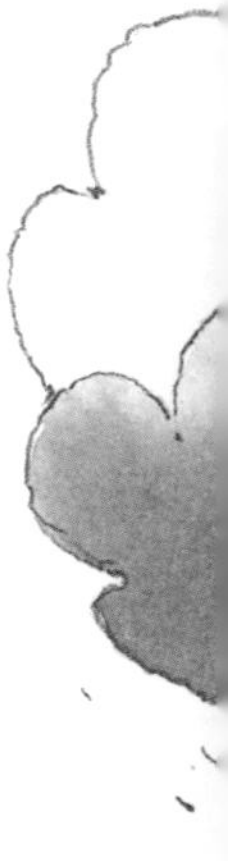

Then Foxy went to the bathroom.
"I mustn't forget to wash my paws," he said.
Then he trotted back to bed.

“Brrr! It’s very cold,” shivered Foxy. He cuddled up with Teddy to get warm.

After a while Foxy felt too hot. He got up and opened the window.

Foxy snuggled down into bed again. He closed his eyes and was nearly asleep when...
"Tweet! Tweet! Tweet!"
All the birds woke up.

"What a long night," yawned Foxy. He began to read his book. Soon he felt very drowsy.

"Zzzz!" At long last Foxy was fast asleep.

"Wake up, sleepy head," said Do
"Get out of bed," said Badger.
But Foxy slept on and on and on

First published in Great Britain by HarperCollins Publishers Ltd in 1995.
ISBN 0 00 761371 7 A CIP catalogue record for this title is available from the British Library.
Printed and bound in Singapore